THIS BLOOMSBURY BOOK

BELONGS TO

Aria

For Nancy xxxxxx – V.F.
To my son, Tim – M.T.

First published in Great Britain in 2006 by Bloomsbury Publishing Plc
36 Soho Square, London, W1D 3QY

Text copyright © Vivian French 2006
Illustrations copyright © Michael Terry 2006
The moral rights of the author and illustrator have been asserted

A CIP catalogue record of this book is available from the British Library

ISBN 0 7475 8267 X (hardback)
ISBN-13 9780747582670

1 3 5 7 9 10 8 6 4 2

ISBN 0 7475 8403 6 (paperback)
ISBN-13 9780747584032

1 3 5 7 9 10 8 6 4 2

All papers used by Bloomsbury Publishing are natural, recyclable products
made from wood grown in well-managed forests. The manufacturing processes
conform to the environmental regulations of the country of origin

Printed in China

Designed by Nina Tara

www.bloomsbury.com

Ellie and Elvis

Vivian French
& Michael Terry

BLOOMSBURY
CHILDREN'S
BOOKS

Ellie and Elvis were best friends.
They both liked bananas.
They both loved oranges.
And they both adored dancing
under the light of the moon ...

"Have some of my banana, Ellie!" said Elvis. "Thank you, Elvis," Ellie said. "And do have some of mine!"

"Can I peel your orange for you, Elvis?" asked Ellie.

Elvis bowed. "As long as you let me give you the biggest slice, Ellie dear."

"HOW beautifully you dance, Ellie!"
Elvis said admiringly.
    Ellie smiled. "HOW handsome you look
when you twirl, Elvis!"

But then, one day, things went
badly wrong ...

Ellie saw Elvis hiding a brown paper bag full of bananas behind a bush ...

... and when she went to look for them later they were gone.

"He must have eaten them all himself," she thought. "ELVIS IS GREEDY!"

Elvis saw Ellie placing a big string
bag of oranges in the crook of a branch ...

... and when he went to look for them later they were gone!

"She must have eaten them all herself," he thought. "Ellie is SELFISH!"

When they went dancing that night
Ellie was thinking so hard about bananas
that she trod on Elvis's toes.

Elvis was thinking so hard about oranges that
he twirled too quickly and knocked Ellie over.
"Elvis," Ellie said as she picked herself up,
"I don't want to dance with you any more."

"That's all right with me,"
Elvis said in a huffy voice.
"I don't want to dance with you either!"

"Don't then," snapped Ellie.
"I won't!" grumped Elvis.

Ellie went off to be by herself under the coconut tree.

And so did ELVIS. They sat back to back, and they didn't say a word.

Then ...

PLOP!

A banana skin plopped on to Ellie's head.

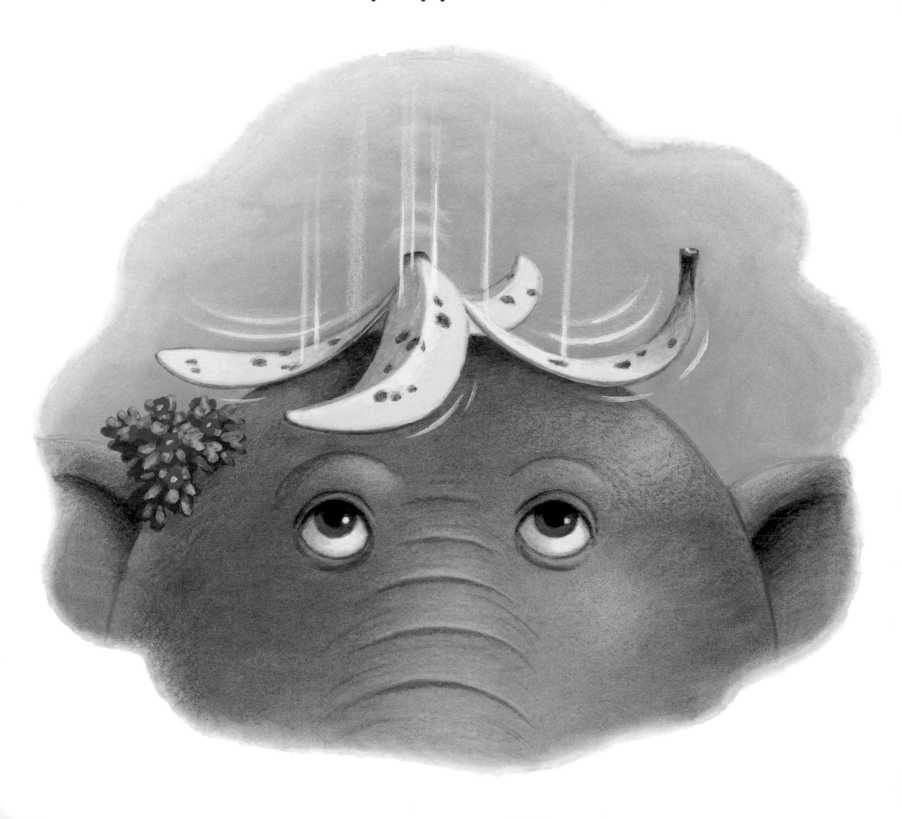

SPLAT!

A half-sucked orange splatted on to Elvis's toes. Ellie and Elvis looked up, and they saw ...

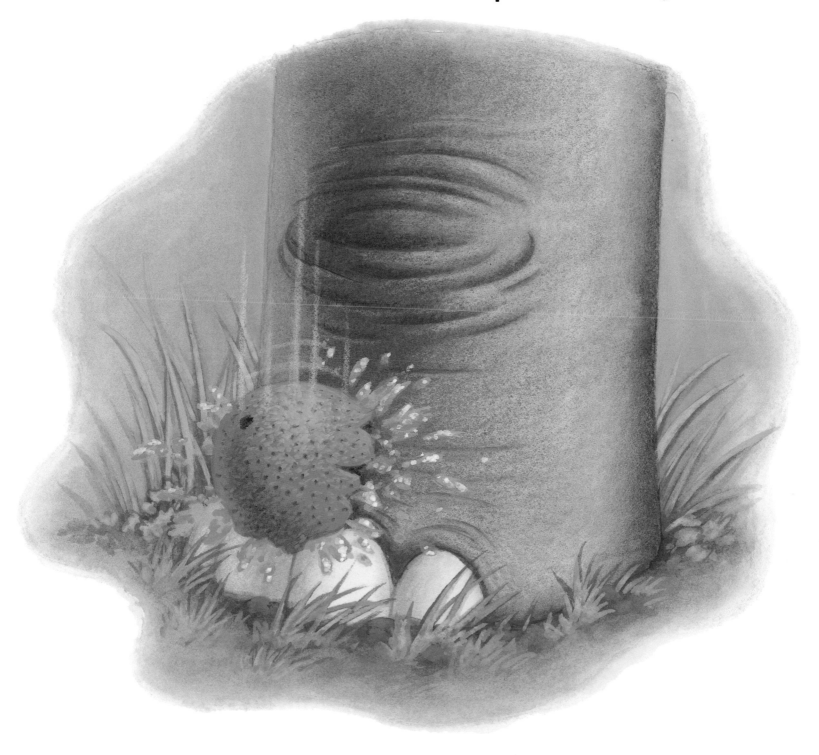

... Mr and Mrs Monkey and seven
little monkeys having a feast
in the coconut tree.

"Those are MY bananas!"
shouted Elvis. "I bought them as
a present for Ellie!"

"And those are MY oranges!"
yelled Ellie. "I bought them
as a present for Elvis!"

"Finders keepers!" shouted the rude little monkeys, and they threw banana skins and orange peel all over Ellie and Elvis.

"Oh, Elvis!" said Ellie. "I'm so sorry! I thought you'd eaten all those bananas yourself!"

"Oh no, Ellie," Elvis said. "They were all for you!" He waggled his trunk, and went rather pink. "I'm sorry too. I thought YOU'D eaten all those oranges."

Ellie gazed at him adoringly.
"They were all for you, dear Elvis,"
she said.
"Ellie," said Elvis, "let's dance!"
"Elvis," said Ellie, "I will dance with
you for ever and ever and EVER!"

Sometimes they stopped dancing
to eat a banana or two ... or an orange.
And they ALWAYS made sure their bananas and
oranges were VERY safe ...

... OR DID THEY?

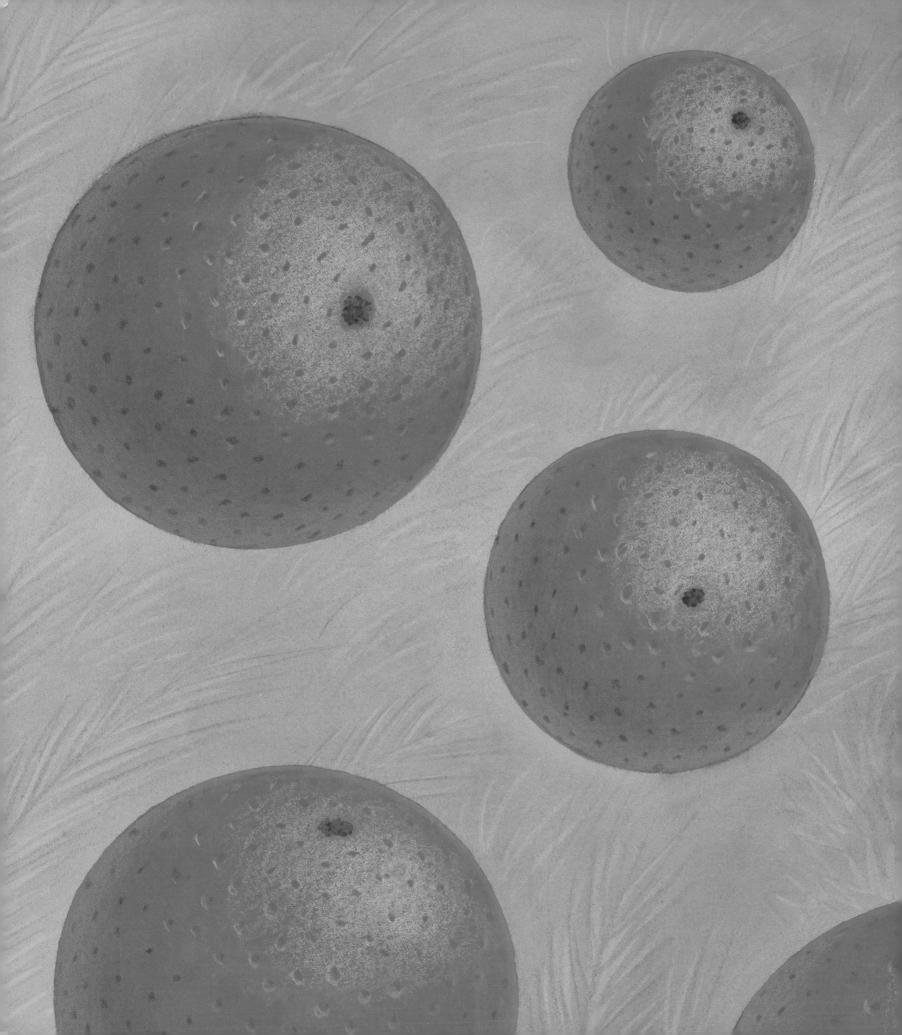

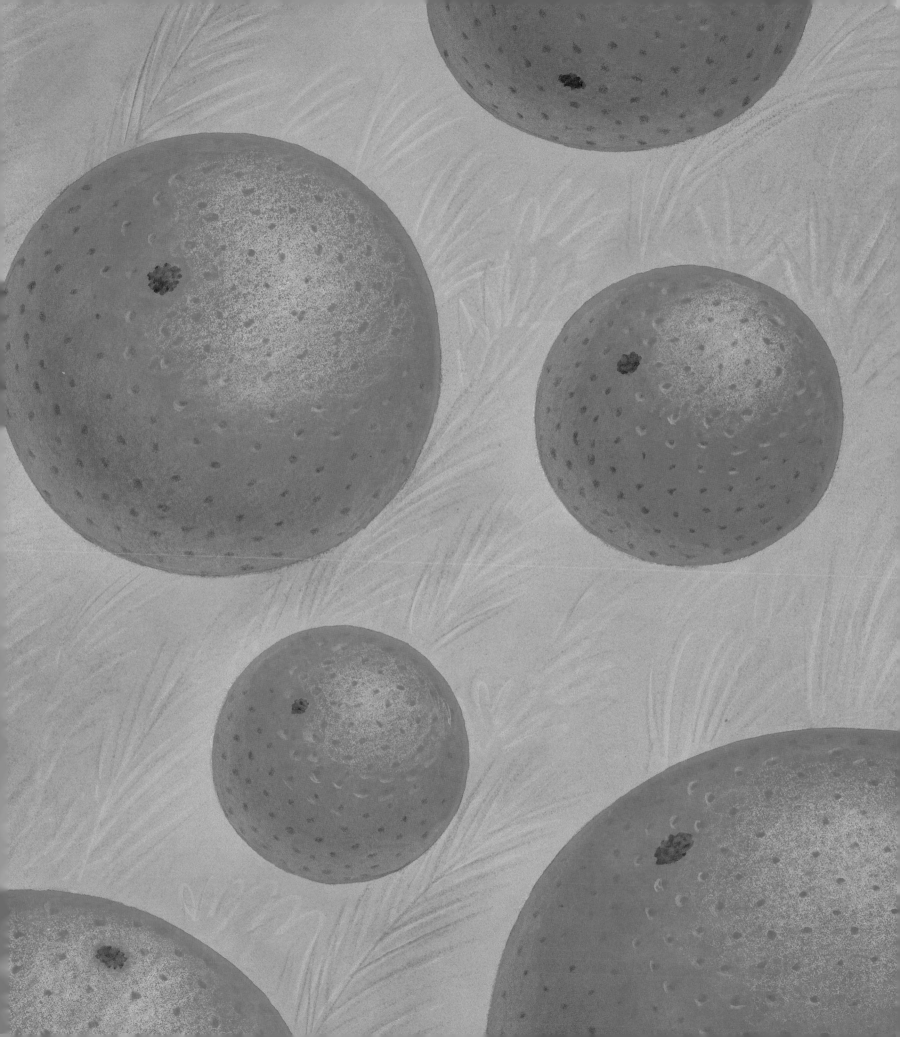